For Love of

Angel

J. Adams

J. Adams

For Love of

Angel

J. Adams

J. Adams

Copyright © 2012, 2015 J. Adams
Jewel of the West Publishing
All Rights Reserved
ISBN-13 978-0692385715
ISBN-10: 0692385711
Library of Congress Control Number: 2015933320
Cover photo by Freedigitalphotos.net

Jewel of the West™
P U B L I S H I N G

To Bailey,
This one is for you

CHAPTER 1

A BIRTHDAY ANGEL

Happy Birthday, Angel!" cry the voices in unison. Angel laughs and claps her hands excitedly as her mommy and daddy begin to sing the birthday song. The rest of the crowd eagerly joins in. Emma and Shane have been looking forward to celebrating their little girl's first birthday all week.

Everyone laughs as Angel plunges into her piece of birthday cake, which now covers her entire face. As Shane Hughes watches his wife try to clean Angel's face, he can't help but think of how blessed they have been to have their little girl in lives.

Shane met Emma in the spring of 1980 at a classical music concert and it was love at first sight.
With her Toffee-colored skin, doe-like eyes, and thick curly hair, she was the most beautiful woman he had ever seen. He was twenty-one and she had just turned twenty. They dated for exactly three weeks before Shane proposed, and they were married one month later. It wasn't long before they were expecting a baby. After moving into a larger apartment in London, Emma started having problems with the pregnancy. She was put on strict bed rest, making the pregnancy seem endless. But months later when their little baby was placed in Emma's arms, all of the problems were forgotten. They decided to name her Angel because she had the most cherubic face either of them had ever seen, and after making it through such a hard pregnancy, they thought it a fitting name for her. Now here they are, celebrating her first year in the world.

"Let's open your presents, Angel," Shane says to his newly cleaned little girl as he scoops up an armful of wrapped packages. He runs to the bedroom and grabs his camera. Before he can even get back to the dining room, Angel has ripped open one of her presents. The Raggedy Ann doll is almost the same size she is. In between pictures, Shane pauses to marvel at how much his little girl looks like her mother. At only a year old, she has a thick mane of dark hair like Emma's and the same beautiful smile. Her skin is light, and her exotic features are a mixture inherited from his Australian blood and Emma's Nigerian. There is even a small mole about an inch away from the corner of her mouth, just like Emma, but she has Shane's blue eyes.

"Dada, Dada," she cries as she holds up the doll for him to see.

"What a pretty doll! Can I be in a picture with you and your doll?"

He hands Emma the camera and Angel smiles as he kneels beside her for the picture.

* * *

After all of the presents have been opened and the guests are gone, Shane puts Angel in her playpen with her new toys and helps Emma clean up.

3

"Let me give you two a hand," Emma's aunt Elaine says, stacking the empty paper cups.

"Thanks," Emma replies, a subtle sadness in her expression.

Reading his wife's thoughts, Shane puts a comforting arm around her.

"Oh, cheer up, you two. You're only going to be gone for a week."

"I know," Shane says, "but we have never left her before."

Elaine smiles at them both. "I know it's hard, but you really need this vacation."

"I suppose," Emma agrees. "But maybe we could–"

"No buts," Elaine interrupts. "I will take good care of her. I promise."

"We know you will," Shane says with complete confidence.

"What time does your plane leave?"

"At 7:05 in the morning."

"Well, then, we had better finish so you can get your last minute things done."

"You know, I really am looking forward to that warm California sun people talk so much about," Emma says, wiping off the counter.

"So am I. We are going to have a great time and bring you back plenty of souvenirs, Elaine."

Elaine grins. "Oh, I'm all for that."

As they talk more about their trip to the United States, Shane can't shake the twinge of sadness he himself has been feeling but has managed not to let show."

Everything will be okay.

* * *

"Oh, I am going to miss you so much!" Emma says as she snuggles her little girl. She holds her for a long moment before handing her to Shane. He takes her in his arms and walks over to one of the large airport windows.

"See that big plane right there? That's the one Mommy and Daddy will be going on."

"Dada," Angel replies, clapping her hands happily.

As the final boarding call came, Shane gives his little girl one last squeeze and returns her to her mother's arms. Emma places a lingering kiss on her forehead before handing her to Elaine.

"I'll take good care of her. Don't worry."

"We know you will," Shane says, wrapping an arm around Emma.

Elaine holds Angel's hand up and helped her wave goodbye as her parents board the plane. They look back and wave until the little girl's face is no longer visible.

* * *

As the plane lifts off the runway, Shane and Emma again assure one another that their daughter will be okay and begin talking about the things they plan to do in California. Shane continues to mask the unexplainable sadness returning to him.

After talking for another hour or two, they sleep for a while. Then they awaken and talk some more. During the quiet moments, Shane is lost in his own thoughts, which are mainly about Angel.

They are soon served a meal and they again quietly speak of their plans as they eat. Looking through the packet of brochures they received a few weeks ago, their excitement is renewed.

Drowsiness finally hits Shane. Glancing over at Emma and finding her sleeping deeply, he decides not to fight it any longer. The rest will do him good. But just as he begins to fall into a light sleep, the sudden jolt of the plane awakens him.

"What was that?" Emma asks sleepily.

"Probably just some turbulence," he assures her. She smiles at him and slowly closes her eyes again.

"Just think, in about seven more hours, I will be sitting on the beach getting a tan with my beautiful wife," he whispered.

Another jolt of the plane awakens Emma completely. This time, the look on Shane's face matches her worried expression.

The sudden flashing of the *Fasten Seat belt* sign starts a stir among the passengers and the urgency in the captain's voice over the intercom telling the passengers to remain seated confirms Shane's suspicion that something is wrong.

"What is it?" Emma asks, her voice shaky.

He takes her hand and holds it against his chest tightly, unable to answer her. He just stares straight ahead. A flight attendant quickly runs by carrying a fire extinguisher. Another emerges from the captain's cabin instructing everyone to remain calm and put on their oxygen mask.

Suddenly the plane lurches downward and the passengers begin to scream. Shane and Emma hold on to each other, crying. Scenes of Angel's birthday party flash through Shane's mind along with scenes of future parties he knows he will never be able to see.

"Help us, God!" are Shane's final words of prayer.

CHAPTER 2

Moving Away

Nineteen years later

She has the most beautiful voice I've ever heard."

"I know. I wish I could sing like that."

I shake my head, smiling as Sharon and Diane listen to me perform my latest song.

"Just look at her fingers move! It's like the keys are a part of her."

"She is at one with the piano."

I laugh, unable to play anymore. Closing song, I receive ecstatic cheers from them both.

"You two are crazy, but you are also the best audience a person could ever have."

"Sharon sighs. "Well, that was the best song you've written yet."

"I totally agree," chimes in Diane. "You will go places with your talent."

"Well, the only place I plan to go is to college in North Carolina."

"Since we are on the subject," Sharon says, wrinkling her nose, "of all the exciting places in the United States, why in the world did you choose North Carolina? You were offered scholarships from California and New York, too."

I smile. "Because UNCA is a very good school with a great music program."

Sharon shoots a skeptical look my way. "So who told you it was a good school?"

I know what her question is leading up to. "Mitch sent me some information on the school and I also spoke with an adviser there. She answered all of my questions."

"Could it be," Sharon presses jokingly, "it's not the school you are going for, but for Mitchell Greenland himself? He's enrolled there getting a degree in architecture, isn't he?"

A heated blush warms my cheeks. *Leave it to Sharon to be so blunt.* "I am going because of the college."

"Ah, come on," Diane quickly adds. "I saw the way you two were at the airport the day he left to go home. You guys were clinging to one another like a koala on a eucalyptus tree. It was easy to see the guy is head over heels for you. And if I'm not mistaken, the feeling is mutual, right?"

I know my face is as scarlet as a plum. "Okay, we have been keeping in touch, but I'm going to North Carolina for the school."

"Uh huh," the two chime together. Then we all giggle like teenagers.

"Well, we had better get going," Diane says, standing up. "My dad is taking us shopping in a bit and he gets pretty testy when he's kept waiting."

I laugh because I know how true that is. Her dad is a stickler for punctuality.

"You want to come with us?"

"No, thanks. I have another song I need to work on, but I'll see you later, okay?"

"Okay, we'll see you."

Moving to the large front window, I watch my friends walk away. It seems I am always doing that. I love spending time with them, but my music is my life and it has been keeping me pretty busy.

Waving a final time, I walk back over to the piano and proceed to play the melody of another song I've been working on, but after a few minutes, I find I can't concentrate.

"Well, I don't think I am going to get anything else done right now." I close the piano lid and placed my music inside the bench. Sighing, I sit in one of the large soft chairs by the window. And just as I have so many times before, I take the white, lace-covered photo album from the table next to the chair. Once again, unbidden tears spring to my eyes as I skim through the pages.

I lightly run my fingers across the picture of my father holding me at the park. I turn the page to a photo of my parents standing with Aunt Elaine. I find it quite sad that my mother and father's parents are all deceased. Both of my father's parents died of cancer, my mother's, in an automobile accident. Having both lost their parents when they were very young, my parents had shared a common bond.

The tears flow freely now as I once again feel a deep longing to have been able to know my own parents, to even remember them at all. Looking through the rest of the photos, my contemplation continues as I take in one of my favorite pictures. It was of me on my first birthday holding the Raggedy Ann doll I received at my party. I always imagine my dad behind the camera, prompting me to smile.

In another photo, my mother and father are holding me. I'm always amazed at how much I look like them. My mother with her long curly hair and brown skin, and my father with his deep blue eyes and big dimples make a very attractive couple. Looking at the photo a few minutes longer, I close the album and placed it back on the table. "I love you both," I whisper softly.

I return to the piano to try and get some more work done on a song when the phone rings.

"Hello."

"Hi, Angel."

My heart skips a beat upon hearing the voice. "Hi, Mitch," I answer, trying to keep my own voice from betraying how excited I am to hear from him. "How are you?"

"I'm great!" I can hear the enthusiasm in his voice. "I'm just so excited about you coming, I couldn't wait to talk to you again. You're on my mind a lot." He still has a mild British accent from the year he spent here studying European architecture.

"I have been thinking about you, too," I tell him, blushing, and I'm glad he can't see me.

"When will you leave?" he asks eagerly.

"One week from today. That way, I will get there a week before registration."

"Good. All of the arrangements have been taken care of. One of the professors at the university is a good friend of mine. He has a very nice rooming house. I rented one of the rooms for you with the money you sent. You're paid up for six months so you won't owe anything until next February."

"Thank you," I say softly. "I can't tell you how much I appreciate all you've done for me."

"I would do anything for you, Angel. I hope you know that."

I smile, hearing the emotion in his voice. "I know you would, and I would do the same for you."I hear him sigh and it warms my heart. "Tell your friend thanks for me. I am looking forward to meeting him."

"You'll like him a lot. He's a very special man, almost like a second father to me."

You're very fortunate. I would give anything to have one father. Instant guilt assaults my heart, brought on by my envious thoughts.

"I have some fun things planned for us to do."

"I can't wait." I long to see him more with each passing day. "I'm almost all packed. All that's left is saying my goodbyes."

"Well, I have been telling everyone here about you and they can't wait to meet you. Especially my family," he adds softly.

"And I can't wait to meet them."

"I guess I'll let you go now. Call me before you leave?"

" I will."

"Until then . . ."

"Until then."

"Goodbye," we say in unison.

* * *

"So, what shall we do tonight?" I ask my aunt.

"Well, I thought we might go out to dinner and maybe a movie, if that's all right."

"It sounds great to me. There are still a few people I need to say goodbye to, but I can do that tomorrow morning before I leave."

"Good. Is that everything?" she asks me as I zip up the last bag.

"I think so." I place a photo of me with Sharon and Diane in another bag. "I can't think of anything–"

"I can," Elaine interrupts. "I will be right back." She quickly returns with the lacy photo album.

"I want you to take this," she says, handing the large book to me. "I always planned to give it to you when you got ready to go out on your own."

Taking the book, I clutch it to my chest. "But you have had this for so long. How can you bear to part with it?"

She sits on the bed next to me. "I had the privilege of raising your mother and I came to know your father so well, I couldn't love him any more if he were my own son. I have their faces engraved in my memory and my heart. They will always be with me."

I hug her tightly. "I am going to miss you so. Thank you."

"I am going to miss you, too. Things will not be the same here without you."

"You will come and see me?"

"You bet. I would like to see America very much." She stands. "I'll leave now and let you finish." When she reaches the door, she turns and says, "Your parents loved you so much. Your father called you his little

Angel." With that, she closes the door, leaving me to my thoughts.

* * *

"It's time to go, Angel. The movie starts at 8:00."

"Coming, Auntie," I call from my room. Examining my reflection once more, I grab my purse. "Okay, I'm ready."

As I exit our flat, I take a moment to study the red brick building that will forever be a part of me. *Oh, how I am going to miss this place!* When my parents died, Aunt Elaine chose to give up her own flat and moved into my parents' to make things easier for me. I have lived here all my life and it is hard to leave. Our home is very elegant, thanks in part to my father's well paying job as an architect, and also because of the savings my parents had put away. I have never wanted for money, but because I still like earning my own money, I give piano lessons.

"Are we going to a different restaurant?" I ask, noticing we are heading in a different direction.

"Yes, as a matter of fact, I thought we might dine at Simpsons tonight. We haven't been there in a long while and I want this to be a special going away dinner for you."

* * *

"I love this place," I tell my aunt as we pull up in front of the restaurant. We quickly find a parking space and go in.

"Hello, I have a reservation. The name is Elaine Althorp."

"Oh, yes," the hostess says. "Right this way."

We follow her to a private room that is closed off to the main part of the restaurant. After the hostess leaves us, I glance at Aunt Elaine and find her smiling widely. As she opens the door, I am greeted by a loud "Surprise!"

"Oh, my goodness!" The room is full of friends and people I have known through the years. I am a little emotional as everyone gathers around me, expressing how much I will be missed. I will definitely miss them all more than words can express.

I hug my aunt. "Thank you so much."

"You're very welcome, dear."

After I take a moment to visit with each person and express my gratitude to all of them for coming, I head to the refreshment table and grab a plate of food. Everything looks wonderful.

"Hi, Angel."

"David." I am surprised to see him.

"How have you been?"

"I've been good. How about you?" I haven't seen David since we stopped dating two years ago. We were both headed in separate directions in life and the break up wasn't an easy one. It had been painful losing his friendship.

"I've been good as well." He silently stares at me for a moment. "Angel, I'm sorry for the way I have treated you. I am so sorry."

Tears fill my eyes. "It's okay, David. I've never held it against you. I have really missed our friendship, though."

"So have I. I feel terrible that it has taken me this long to realize just how important your friendship is to me."

Reaching across the table, I squeeze his hand. "It has been a long time."

"I got you something." He reaches into his jacket pocket and pulls out a small wrapped box.

"David, you didn't have to bring me anything."

"I know," he says with a smile. "Just open it."

I unwrap the box. "David, this is so beautiful!" Inside is a silver heart-shaped locket. A small rose is engraved on the front.

"There are places inside to put pictures of you and the guy who is finally fortunate enough to win your heart."

I walk around the table and hug him. "Thank you, David. I will treasure it always."

"You're very welcome." He gives my hand a squeeze. "Well, I guess I had better go. I have a job interview this evening."

"That's great."

"Thanks. Good luck to you, Angel. I wish you all the best."

"And I wish nothing but good things for you," I tell him, wiping a tear away. "I'll keep in touch, all right?"

He nods, then meekly kisses my cheek and leaves.

I stand a minute longer, pondering how much I will miss David, as well as my other friends.

"What's wrong, honey?" Aunt Elaine asks. She pulls out a handkerchief and wipes the tears I missed.

"Nothing. I'm just so grateful for each person here."

Drying my face a final time, I grab my plate and rejoin the crowd. I spend the rest of the evening opening goodbye presents and sharing memories I've made with these amazing friends through the years.

When it is time to say goodbye, I am unable to hold back the tears as I am showered once again with hugs and good wishes.

* * *

The next morning

"Oh, I am going to miss you so much," Elaine says giving Angel one last squeeze.

"I will miss you, too. I promise to write you every chance I get."

"And I will write to you."

As Elaine watches her niece board the plane, it brings back the painful memories of Shane and Emma. She never dreamed when she waved goodbye to them that day that it would be the last time she would see them alive.

God, she silently prays, *please, take care of my baby. Please, keep her safe.*

* * *

As I sit looking out over the ocean, I wonder if my parents had the same feelings of anticipation and excitement of going to America that I'm having now. For me, not only is the thought of living in America exciting, but also the thought of being with Mitch. I couldn't let myself admit to my friends just how deep my feelings are for him. I smile as I remember how excited he was when I called him the day before yesterday to let him know what time my flight will arrive.

"My plane is scheduled to arrive in Asheville on Wednesday afternoon at 2:20 your time."

"I can't wait to see you. I've missed you so much."

"I've missed you, too," I say, *trying not to sound as ecstatic as I feel.*

"Then I will see you Wednesday."

I can tell he doesn't want to hang up. And neither do I. *"I'll see you Wednesday, Mitch . . . Goodbye."*

Every time I've had to end a call with him, I have felt lonely afterward. Now I'll be able to see him every day and really share my feelings with him. I know that once we are together, I will never feel alone again.

CHAPTER 3

IAN

*H*earing a familiar voice calling my name, I scan the baggage claim area.

"Mitch," I call to him as his handsome form emerges from the crowd. Running to him, I throw my arms around his neck. "Oh, it's so good to see you!"

"It's good to see you, too!"

He takes my carry-on bag and tosses it over his shoulder. Taking my hand, he leads me through the crowd.

"How was your flight?"

"It was really long, but fun."

We grab my luggage and haul it out on a rented cart. Soon we have the bags loaded in the car and are on our way.

I marvel at how beautiful North Carolina is. It's as humid as London, but I don't mind. Mitch tells me I couldn't have picked a better time of year to come. The hot summer is starting to cool down and the weather is nice and mild.

"What do you think?" he asks me as we drive through downtown Asheville."

"It's lovely. And I've been looking forward to visiting the Biltmore House," I say as we pass the entrance to the scenic drive leading to the mansion.

"I can't wait to take you there, and so many other places." He gives my hand a squeeze, keeping it in his as he drives.

* * *

"This is Biltmore Forest," he tells me as we drive through the tree-clad streets. "The rooming house is not too far."

"This is a very pretty area. The name fits. It really looks like a forest, and it seems very prominent."

"It is. A lot of the home owners are doctors, lawyers, and some of them are just plain rich."

"Well, I absolutely love it."

Mitch smiles at me. "I thought you would."

We finally stop in front of a large Tudor-styled house.

"This is it."

"It's beautiful." When he doesn't respond, I turn to find him staring me.

"*You* are beautiful."

The compliment catches me off guard and I don't know what to say. "Thank you." Unable to resist, I lean over and kiss his cheek. We silently stare at one another for a moment before getting out of the car.

Mitch knocks firmly. A minute later the door is opened by an elderly woman.

"Hi, Ms. Crawford. How are you today?"

"Oh, I'm just fine, Mitchell. Come on in." Mitch holds the door open for me. We follow the woman to the large family room.

"Please, have a seat."

Mitch thanks her. "This is Angel. She is going to be living here."

"Oh, yes, I have heard a lot about you. I am Louise Crawford, Ian's mother. I'm glad to finally be able to meet you." She gives Mitch a wink and I smile, pretending not to notice.

"It's good to meet you, too."

"Ian had to step out for a moment. I'm sure he will be back soon. Can I get you something to drink while you wait?"

"No, thank you," Mitch answers. "How about you, Angel?"

"No, nothing for me, thank you."

"Well, why don't you show Angel around the place. I have to go to the store and pick up a few groceries, so I will leave you two."

"We'll be fine," Mitch assures her.

Smiling, Louise takes her purse from the coat rack and leaves.

"She is a really sweet lady," Mitch tells me as he watches her pull out of the driveway.

"She seems very nice. Does she live here, too?"

"No, actually she lives in a condo a couple of streets over. About five years ago, Ian's father died, so he bought this place to be closer to his mother. He fell in love with it the moment he saw it, and because it was so big, he decided to rent out some of the rooms. Until you came, there were only two other tenants. You will really like Ian and I'm sure you will like living here."

"I'm pretty sure I will too," I agree.

Mitch gives me a tour of the first floor of the house. We are in the kitchen when we hear the front door open.

"That's probably Ian. You wait here and I'll go and get him."

"All right."

* * *

"Mitch," Ian says as he meets him in the hallway. "How are you?"

"I'm great. I brought a new tenant for you."

Ian can tell by the wide smile on Mitch's face who the tenant is. "She's here?"

"Yes."

"Where is she?" Ian asks eagerly.

"She's in the kitchen. Come on."

* * *

Standing in front of the large kitchen window, I stare out at the beautiful landscape. In a way, Asheville reminds me of home, and I suddenly find myself missing Aunt Elaine.

The kitchen is heavenly. It's so big and full of light. I wander into the attached garden room. In the center there is a lavender floral couch and chair, and two lovely wicker end tables. Various green plants in decorative planters inhabit the corners. The ceiling is also glass, so it looks as though the whole room is outside, and I am sure this will be my favorite room in the house.

"Angel," Mitch calls.

"I'm in here."

"I see you have found my place of retreat."

I turn to see the face belonging to the voice, and for a second, I am startled. But only for a second. Extending my hand, I greet him with a smile.

"It's good to meet you, Angel. You did very well, you know. Most people don't know what to say when they first see me."

I hadn't meant for him to notice, but he had. It had been hard not to react when I saw his face.

* * *

Ian understands her reaction. His skin had been badly burned, and even the numerous skin grafts he'd undergone hadn't made it look any better. Through the years he has grown to accept his appearance. And those closest to him have accepted it as well.

"It's wonderful to meet you, too, Mr. Crawford," Angel finally says.

Ian smiles. He can tell she is embarrassed by her initial reaction. It had been involuntary, but it is obvious she feels bad. He laughs, wanting to put her at ease. "Well, if you are going to live here, the first thing you must do is stop calling me Mr. Crawford. Call me Ian."

Angel smiles. "Okay, Ian."

"We are going to get along great," he says cheerfully. "Now, come with me and I will show you to your room."

"Thank you."

* * *

Mitch goes to get my luggage while Ian leads me upstairs.

"This is an amazing house," I tell him.

"Thank you. I love it, too."

On the way up, I stop and ask him questions about the photos on the wall. "This is beautiful," I say, staring at one of a large field of flowers.

"Yes, this is one of my favorites also."

While Ian talks about the things he loves about the picture, I take in his features. His blond wavy hair, streaked with a little gray, is neatly cut and his eyes are a sparkling blue. As we talk, I decide what is most attractive about him is his spirit. It seems to radiate from him, so much so that after a while, I don't even notice his face.

"So, what kinds of things did you do in England?" he asks as we reach the top of the stairs.

"Well, I've never been one to go out much. I'm sort of a homebody."

Ian grins. "Sounds a lot like myself. But surely you must have things you enjoy doing."

"Oh, yes," I say, blushing slightly. "I give piano lessons and I like to write songs. I am also a big fan of old black and white movies."

"Really? So am I."

"I've spent a lot of late nights in front of the television."

"This is wonderful! I have a large collection of old classics. Maybe we could watch a few sometime."

I smile. His excitement is contagious. "I would like that a lot."

When we reach my room, he opens the door and moves back, allowing me to enter.

"Oh, wow! This is beautiful." I have never seen such a pretty bedroom. The bedding is white satin and lace with matching drapes. The carpet is a plush, light gray and there is a small, round glass bistro table with two chairs in a corner. On the table sits a large crystal vase of red and white roses. On the dresser stands a beautiful porcelain doll in a wedding dress and another vase of roses. There is also a private bathroom. It is truly a dream room.

"I'm glad you like it. I decorated this room myself and until now, it has never been used."

I find myself wondering why he decorated the room this way. It is clear to me he cherishes it, and it's also clear he is pleased that I like it. "I feel honored to be the first to stay in here," I tell him sincerely.

"The honor is all mine," he says, looking at me for a long moment. "Now, I'll go and help Mitch bring up your luggage."

"Thank you."

I stare after him for a long moment. I've only known this man for a few moments, yet I feel a connection to him I can't explain. Walking around the room, I take in the various details, and with each thing I come across, I find myself wondering what made him choose that particular object.

"We're back," Mitch announces.

"Thank you." They put the bags next to the bed.

"You are most welcome," Ian says with a smile.

Mitch takes my hand in his. "I'm going to leave and let you get settled." I notice Ian quietly leaving the room to give us a minute alone. "I'll come back this evening to take you out and show you the town, okay?"

"Okay." I hope I don't sound as reluctant to let him go as I feel. I can't stand the thought of being away from him, even for a little while, but I do need to get unpacked.

"I'll pick you up at 6:30." Giving me a smile that completely melts my heart, he kisses my cheek and leaves.

* * *

I start unpacking my things. Taking out the photo album, I place it on the bottom shelf of the nightstand next to the bed, and then I fill the drawers with my clothes. Half an hour later, I am finally done. Just as I place the picture of Sharon, Diane and me on the table, there is a soft knock on the door.

"Come in."

Ian sticks his head in. "Am I interrupting you?"

"No, not at all. Please, come in."

Opening the door wider, he looks around. "It look like you're all settled. Everything looks really nice."

"Thank you, but it's easy with the way you've decorated."

He smiles. "So, what do you think of North Carolina so far?"

"I think it's beautiful."

"So do I."

I sit on the bed and invite him to sit down as well. He pulls the chair from the small desk.

"So, how long have you been teaching at the university?" I ask.

"For about five years now."

"From what Mitch tells me, you are a very good literature professor. How did you get into it?" I watch him absently rub his hands together.

"It was something I was always interested in."

Ian has a quiet way about him that I like a lot. I study him a moment longer before sensing that I am making him nervous. "I'm sorry," I tell him. "I don't mean to stare. It's just that you have very beautiful eyes.

I can't help looking at them. They remind me of my father's eyes in the photos I have of him."

"Thank you," he says softly. "Mitch told me you lost your parents when you were young. I was very sorry to hear that."

"Thank you. I only wish I had been able to know them."

"I'm sure they loved you very much."

"I feel they did." I am touched by the tenderness in his voice. "May I ask you something?"

"Sure."

"How did you get burned?" When he looks away, instant guilt fills me. "I am sorry. That was too personal, wasn't it?"

"No, it's just that it happened a long time ago and I try not to think about it."

"I am really sorry," I say again. "I didn't mean to pry."

"It's okay." He quickly stands. "Well, I will leave you to rest up a bit. Is there anything you need?"

"No, everything is fine. Thank you."

"You're most welcome."

As he turned to go, I touch his sleeve. "I am truly sorry for being so personal."

"Believe me," he says with a smile, "it's okay."

* * *

Closing the door to Angel's room, Ian quickly walks to his own. Once the door is closed, the emotion he'd managed to hold back rushes to the surface. Moving to the bed, he sits down, buries his face in his hands and cries.

She's so beautiful! She looks just like her mother. My Angel is so beautiful! He cries until he can't anymore.

When there is a soft knock at the door, he quickly wipes his face. Before he can answer, Louise enters.

Closing the door, she rushes to his side. "What is it? What's wrong?" There is panic in her voice.

Ian looks at her through swollen red eyes, his heart pounding harder. "Mother," he says softly, "I have something I need to tell you. But I need you to agree not to interrupt me until I have finished."

* * *

"All right," Louise agrees, sitting next to him.

Ian turns to face her and prays for the strength to get through this.

"You have truly been the best mother I could have ever asked for. You and Father took me into your lives and loved me as though you had raised me. I will always be grateful to you for that. I can never repay you for the joy you have given me, and for the privilege of being your son after not having a mother and father for so long."

Looking into her eyes, he knows her thoughts because she has spoken the words many times– that it was they who were blessed to have found a son after losing their own–but she doesn't interrupt him.

"When you were assigned to be my nurse in the hospital, I was so lost. And when I had no memory of who I was or what had happened, you were there for me. Father was the most caring doctor I had ever known."

"He was a good man," Louise says, solemnly.

"I remember when you told me there had been a plane crash and there were no survivors. Because of a computer glitch, part of the airline manifest for that flight was lost."

Louise nods. "Yes, I remember too. Later that same evening, you were found by some fishermen, lying on the shore. You had no memory of who you were and no one would ever have guessed you could be a passenger from that flight because it was so far away."

Ian smiles sadly. "I remember you both bandaging my burned face and chest. You were always there to take care of me. A year had passed before I totally regained my memory. You helped me through the shock of realizing that I had lost my wife. And even though I had my memory back, you both loved me so much, you urged me to stay and be a part of your family."

Louise smiles at him through tear-filled eyes. "You had become a son to us. We felt God had sent you to us. Your father wanted someone to carry on his name. We thought since you were an only child and you had no family back in England, it wouldn't matter if you took our name."

Ian swallows hard, his nerves starting to cave in. He knows what he is about to say will shock his mother, and he prays she will be able to forgive him. He looks down at his trembling hands and presses them together, trying to make them stop. Louise takes them in hers.

"What is it Ian? You can tell me anything."

Tears again fill his eyes. "Mother, I wasn't totally truthful to you and Father." He hesitates and takes another deep breath. "I told you I didn't have any other family in England, but . . . I lied."

Louise's mouth drops open slightly and Ian senses her struggling to remain calm. But she stays silent, hearing him out.

"There was my wife's aunt." He pauses, running a shaky hand through his hair. "And with her was a little girl; a beautiful little girl. She . . . she's my daughter."

Louise covers her mouth, her eyes widening, and silently listens as he tells her about his daughter and the last day he saw her.

During a pause, Louise finally speaks. "But why would . . . why would you let your daughter grow up believing you were dead? How could . . ." She didn't finish. Covering her face with her hands, she silently cries.

Ian pulls her hands away, lifting her chin, and then points to his face. "This is why." Tears roll down his cheeks. "How would she have felt being raised by someone who looked like this? What kind of life would she have had? To most people I look like a freak."

"Ian, don't," she interrupts.

"Mother, it's true. Just look at me. How could I do that to her? She wouldn't have had a normal life with me. But I knew she would if my wife's aunt raised her." He closes his eyes tightly. "When the day came that I finally remembered everything, it was then that I decided to permanently change my name to Ian. I had to rid myself of the past, which meant I couldn't be Shane Hughes anymore. Each and every time I looked at my face, I became more convinced that he didn't exist anymore. Maybe it was a mistake, but I did it for my daughter, and it is too late to do anything about it. She's made a life without me and I don't want to cause her any more heartache."

"But, Ian, you are her father."

"I've thought of nothing but her for years. Not a day goes by that I don't ache to hold her, to love her, but

I can't. She deserves better. Better than what I can give her."

Louise touches his face. "You can give her love, Ian. You can give her that."

He shakes his head as tears continue to wet his scarred face. "You know, I used Mitch to get her here. I'm not proud of it, but I did. He doesn't know anything. From the moment I received his letter telling me about her, about this special girl that had captured his heart, I just knew I had to see her. So I convinced him to talk to her about coming here to go to school. I told him I would rent her a room. That way I could see her and get to know her without revealing who I really was to her. I spent days remodeling her room, wanting everything to be just right."

"You mean the sweet girl I met today . . . She's your daughter?"

"Yes, Angel is my daughter."

For a moment, Louise's mouth moves, but nothing comes out. "Oh, Ian," she says sadly.

"I was desperate, Mother!" he cries. "I just wanted to be near her."

"I know," she says softly. "I know." She wipes her eyes, silently contemplating what her son just shared.

Ian feels as if a large weight has been removed from his chest. It has been hard keeping this secret for so many years. He knows he has hurt his mother deeply. Taking her hand, he kisses the back of it, holding it to his chest.

"Mother, I beg you to forgive me for keeping this from you. I know you don't think my reasons are good ones, but I really felt I was doing the best thing for her. Please forgive me."

Louise hugs him. "I forgive you. I know you were doing what you thought was best. But now that she is here, you need to tell her."

Ian shakes his head. "I can't."

A tiny smile creeps across Louise's face. Then to Ian's surprise, she chuckles. "Oh, Ian, don't you see? This is all a part of God's plan. It wasn't mere chance that Mitch met Angel when he went to England. God led him to her, and He knows you need to be free of this secret. You need to be forgiven, not just by me, but by your daughter as well. God brought the two of you together. You must let her know who you are."

Ian drops his head into his hands. He knows she is right, but he just doesn't think he can do it. It would hurt her so much and that is the last thing he wants to do.

"She will hate me," he says quietly. "Right now, at least I have a chance to be her friend. If I tell her the truth, she will hate me and see me for the monster I truly am. I need her friendship. I can't risk losing that opportunity."

Louise pats his hand gently. "It's true she might be angry with you at first, but she will eventually understand the love that went into your decision. It's a chance you are going to have to take, because you don't just need her friendship, you need her to be your daughter. And she doesn't know it yet, but she needs you, too."

Ian shrugs. "I just don't know."

"I know you're afraid, son. But the moment I met her, I could tell she was a good person, and I know in my heart she will forgive you. You just have to give her the chance."

He nods slowly. "You're right. I am afraid. I ache to hold my daughter in my arms and let her know I'm her father. I'm just . . . I'm just so scared. I don't want to lose her. I would rather die."

"Ian, I want you to do something for me."

"Anything."

"Tonight, when you say your prayers, I want you to pray about Angel. Ask God to give you strength and help you to set things right with her. Ask for help to know what to say and when to say it. You will know when the time is right. I know you will. Will you do that for me?"

Choking back a sob, Ian nods. "Yes."

CHAPTER 4

ANGEL'S FIRST NIGHT

Standing in front of the full-length mirror, I straighten the collar of my blouse. The blue vertical stripes make me look even taller than my five-foot-seven inch frame. I pair it with navy slacks. I want to look nice, but not too dressy, and this is the perfect outfit. Just as I finish spreading some gloss on my lips, there is a soft knock on the door. I quickly open it, excited spend the evening with Mitch.

Mitch's wide smile produces butterflies inside me. In his hands is a box of Godiva chocolates. "These are for you."

"You didn't have to . . ."

"I wanted to. Besides, I know how much you love chocolate and this is some of the best."

"Thank you." Taking the box, I kiss his cheek.

"Well, I guess I'll have to bring you candy more often."

I laugh. "Just one minute. Let me get my purse."

"You look great," he tells me as I close the door.

"Thanks. So do you." The peach-colored oxford shirt and tan Dockers look perfect on him. His dark wavy hair is wind blown, making him look as handsome as ever.

We meet Ian at the bottom of the stairs. In his hands is a steaming mug of hot chocolate. He and Mitch greet each other and Mitch tells him what we have planned for the evening. As they talk, I again find myself staring at Ian, still unable to understand why I am so drawn to him.

"We'll probably go for a walk through the college gardens," I hear Mitch say, drawing me from my thoughts.

"You are going to love the gardens," Ian tells me.

"I'm looking forward to it," I say with a smile, looking up at him. He smiles back and follows us to the door.

"You two have a good time," Ian calls as Mitch opens the car door for me. I wave as we drive away.

* * *

Ian stands in the doorway long after they leave, lost in thought.

If we were father and daughter, he sadly muses, *I could have given her a hug and kissed her cheek before she left. I could have said to Mitch, "Be careful with my daughter," and told her I loved her.* He closes his eyes tightly, leaning his head against the door frame.

"But she *is* my daughter."

* * *

Mitch takes me for a drive around the city, then we tour the university campus. I am awed by how big the school is and I look forward to my first day there. After the tour, we take a walk through the college's botanical gardens.

As we sit on one of the wooden benches, I feel an overwhelming sense of gratitude for being here, especially being here with Mitch. I turn to him and smile and he puts an arm around me, drawing me close. I soak in the warmth of his embrace as he shares funny stories of his childhood and what it was like growing up with five sisters. I in turn share more about my own childhood. I enjoy this time talking with him and learning new things about each other.

After we leave the school gardens, Mitch takes me out to dinner. We decide to have Mexican, which is a real treat for me. I have never tasted anything so good in my life, and by the time we are done, I am so full, I'm sure I won't need to eat for the next couple of days.

It isn't long before we are pulling into Ian's driveway.

"I had a great time," he says, opening the car door for me.

"I did, too. Thanks so much for taking me."

"It was my pleasure."

Taking my hand, he walks me to the door. I don't want this night to end and I can tell he feels the same. We stand on the porch for a moment looking at each other. Then Mitch draws me close and kisses me gently. I've dreamed of kissing Mitch a thousand times, and I've tried to imagine how it would be, but as his arms circle my waist and the warmth of the kiss increases, I know with absolute certainty that my dreams of being the recipient of his affections pale in comparison to the real thing.

He draws back slowly. "I guess I should go now," he whispers.

"I know. Me too," I say, not letting go of his hand.

"Can I call you tomorrow afternoon?"

"Of course you can."

Pulling me close again, he favors me with another warm kiss, then forces himself to leave.

Sighing, I watch him drive away before going inside. Noticing a light coming from the living room, I enter and find Ian sitting on the couch watching *Casablanca*.

"May I join you?" I ask.

"Sure. Have a seat." He moves one of the large pillows and I sit next to him.

"Would you like some popcorn," he asks, extending the bowl to me.

"Oh, no thank you. I ate so much for dinner tonight, I feel like I am going to explode."

He chuckles. "Let me guess, Mexican, right?"

"How did you know?"

"Because, every time I eat Mexican I have to be brought out in a wheel barrel."

"I can believe it," I say, laughing. "I've never had Mexican food before tonight. It was very good."

"It's one of my favorite foods."

"I think it's mine now, too."

We turn our attention to the movie. Every now and then Ian makes a comment using his "Bogie" impression, making me laugh, and I crack him up with my Ingrid Bergman impersonation. After a while, we are both laughing so hard, we can't even finish the movie. We eventually turn the television off and talk for a while.

* * *

Ian rakes a hand back through his blond waves. "So, tell me about your two friends in London. Diane and Sharon is it?"

"Yes," she answers. "They are two of the most amazing friends I could ever ask for. I have known them since I was fourteen. We've always been close, and when it comes to my song writing, they were, and still are my biggest fans."

"It must be wonderful to have friends like that. I'll bet you miss them very much."

She sighs. "I do, but I miss my Aunt Elaine even more."

Ian decides to take advantage of this opportunity and learn more about Elaine. It has been a long time and he has thought of her often. "Mitch told me she raised you. She must be a very special lady." He remembers how close he and Emma were to her.

"She is," Angel agrees. "She has been both mother and father to me. I will always be grateful to her for raising me the way she did."

So will I. "Your parents would be very proud of you," he says softly.

"I hope so. I never knew them, but I still miss them. I miss being able to talk to them, learning from them, being loved by them."

Ian swallows hard at the lump in his throat. He never thought losing them would be so painful for her. She was only a baby then. How can she still miss them so much? He pauses, wanting to say something comforting. "I'm sure your parents tried to give you a lifetime of love in the little time they had with you." Saying this makes his heart ache for her even more.

* * *

I swallow against the rising emotion, blinking back the tears. "I know you're probably right, but sometimes it's . . . it's just so hard." I heave a deep sigh, noticing that Ian has become quiet. "I'm sorry for getting emotional. I don't know what's wrong with me these days."

"It's all right, really." But the sadness I see in his blue eyes says otherwise.

Grateful for his listening ear, I place my hand on his. "I'm sorry I upset you."

Ian lifts his teary gaze to mine and I am touched by the emotion I see in his eyes. I wish so badly that I could read his thoughts.

"It's not you," he says. "I just have a lot on my mind." When a tear rolls down his face, I automatically reach out and wipe his cheek, ignoring the stinging in her own eyes. He reaches up and covers my hand with his, holding it against his face. I can feel the uneven texture of his skin beneath my fingers, but I have no desire to pull away. I only feel more drawn to him.

"I'm sorry," he finally says. "I didn't mean to get so emotional." He smiles. "I promise you I'm not unstable."

"It's all right," I tell him as he releases my hand. "I don't know what you are going through, but it must be something very painful."

"It is," he says softly.

"I know we've only met today, but I feel like I have known you forever, and I'm not sure why. If you ever need to talk, I'm a good listener."

He smiles. "Thank you. Maybe one day I will take you up on that."

"Well, I guess I will turn in now," I say, standing.

"It is pretty late. I think I will, too."

"Are you sure you are all right?" I ask him.

"Don't worry about me, Angel. I'm fine." He stands, then reaches for my hand, squeezing it once more. "Thank you for talking with me, and for caring."

I give him a warm smile. "You're welcome. Anytime."

I start up the stairs to my room. Ian quickly turns out the light and follows me up. "Angel?"

"Yes?" I pause, turning to him.

* * *

"Do you and Mitch have any plans for tomorrow?"

"Not really. Mitch is working until later in the afternoon. Why?"

"Well, I was planning to pack a lunch tomorrow and go for a drive up Blue Ridge Parkway. Would . . . would you like to come with me?" He hopes he doesn't sound as desperate as he feels inside. He wants to spend all of the time he can with her without intruding on her time with Mitch.

"I would love to," she answers.

"Great. We can leave around ten, if that's okay."

Angel nods. "That sounds good. I look forward to it."

"Me, too."

"Well, goodnight then."

"Goodnight, Angel. Sleep well."

"You too."

Ian gets ready for bed, but he is still too wound up to sleep. Staring at the moon through his bedroom window, he ponders the special time he just shared with Angel. The emotion that passed between them had been unexpected and he feels blessed to have had those moments with her.

When he finally does get into bed, he finds it difficult to sleep. Thoughts of spending the day with his daughter tomorrow consume him and he is both excited and nervous.

Just as his mind calms enough to sleep, he remembers his promise to his mother. He gets up and kneels beside the bed in the dark. He is used to praying and has never let a day go by without talking to God. But this time is different. This time he is praying about something that will forever change his life and the life of the one person he loves more than anything.

CHAPTER 5

IAN'S DAY WITH ANGEL

As Ian drives up the parkway, I take in the beautiful scenery, marveling at the leafy trees and their various shades of red, orange, yellow and green, and I decide the pictures in the North Carolina brochures Mitch sent me last month don't do it justice. I glance at Ian in wonder and he smiles, and I'm sure he is sensing my thoughts.

"I often drive up here when I need to be alone, or sometimes to just sit and think."

"I can see why. This is incredible!"

Reaching Ian's favorite spot, we pull off the side of the road by a small hidden stream. "This is beautiful," I sigh.

Ian nods. "I think this is the most peaceful spot up here." He grabs the picnic basket from the back seat and we walk through the trees, stopping at some large rocks by the stream. The temperature is a little cool but not uncomfortably so.

While Ian unpacks the basket, I close my eyes, lean back against the rock and tilt my face up toward the sun. *The sun in London never felt like this.* I relish the warmth on my face.

* * *

Ian stops unpacking the basket and watches Angel, remembering the days long ago when he would lie out on the grass with her while she crawled back and forth over his chest. He would spend the entire day playing with her until they both tired themselves out. Afterward, Angel always rested her head on his chest and they'd both fall asleep.

The memory of that time makes his heart ache and he presses a hand to his chest, as if it might calm the pain. When Angel opens her eyes and meets his intent gaze, he quickly returns to unpacking the basket. "So, what are you majoring in, as if I need to ask."

She smiles, turning to him. "Music."

"Maybe I can convince you to perform something for me sometime."

"I would love to."

Ian pours a couple of cups of lemonade and hands one to Angel, noticing her hands as she lifts the cup to take a drink. Her long, slender fingers are very graceful looking. *Just like her mother's hands.*

* * *

"What is your favorite type of music?" I ask him.

"I love ballads and blues. They have been my favorites almost all of my life."

"They are mine, too."

"Seems like we have a lot in common," he says, smiling. I smile back, pleased that we share so many of the same interests.

Ian hands me a sandwich. We quietly eat, listening to the sound of the wind rustling the leaves on the trees. Not much else is said between us. We just silently enjoyed one another's company.

Before leaving, we take a walk along the stream, occasionally passing by patches of wildflowers. I stop and pluck a few off the stems and toss them on the water. Watching them float down the stream, I contemplate the man walking beside me. He a mystery that I need to unravel–that I feel *driven* to unravel.

"Ian, may I asked you something?"

"Sure."

"Have you ever been married?" I can tell my question has caught him off guard. My aunt has always told me I have a way of doing that to people.

"I was once. But, it didn't last very long."

"I'm sorry," I say, assuming he means divorce. "Do you think you will ever get married again, and maybe have children?"

"I don't know, Angel," he softly answers. It is a full minute before he speaks again. "I don't know if anyone will ever be able to get past this," he says, gesturing to his face. "I never thought getting married again was an option. Besides, I wouldn't want to put my child through that. He or she would never be able to have a normal childhood."

Startled by his answer, I reach for his hand, pulling him to a stop, and look into his earnest eyes. "How can you think that? Any woman would consider herself lucky to have you. And your children would be blessed to have you as their father. If anything, your courage and strength would be a strength to them." I pause, surprised at the intensity of my feelings. "I would give anything to have my father here."

* * *

Tears burn Ian's eyes and he quickly blinks them back. He can literally feel her pain, and even though he longs to say, *"Oh, my Angel, your father is right here,"* he is still too afraid. "Thank you, Angel," is all he manages to voice.

Since Ian has some things he needs to take care of and Angel is expecting a call from Mitch, they decide to head back. She helps him pack everything into the basket and he puts it in the back seat. Getting into the car, they head back to the city.

"We'll have to do this again," Ian tells Angel as he holds the screen door open for her.

"I would like that a lot."

"Angel . . . I don't mean to put you on the spot or anything, but I was wondering if you would sing something for me."

She smiles. "I would love to."

Walking over to the piano, Angel sits on the bench and slides over, making room for Ian to sit next to her.

"This old thing hasn't been played in a long time," he tells her. "I hope it's still in tune."

She plays a few keys. "It still sounds pretty good." She takes a moment to loosen up her fingers. "All right, what would you like to hear?"

"You pick something," he says, excited to hear anything she chooses to perform.

Pausing to think for a moment, she begins to sing "Summertime," an old Broadway tune. Ian remembers the song well. Never has he heard anything as beautiful as Angel singing. She does a medley of classics from

Barbara Streisand and the Carpenters, ending with the hymn, "How Great Thou Art."

Ian is silent for a moment. When he finally speaks, his voice cracks. "You have a gift Angel, a very beautiful gift."

"Thank you," she says shyly, giving him a warm smile.

* * *

The phone rings and Ian hurries to answer it. "It's for you," he tells me as I enter the kitchen. "It's Mitch." Whispering his thanks for the songs, he hands me the phone and leaves to give me some privacy.

"Hello, Mitch." I am delighted to hear from him so soon.

"How has your day been?" he asks. " I hope you weren't too bored."

"No, actually I had a great day."

"Really? What did you do?"

"I went for a drive up the parkway with Ian and we had a picnic."

"That's great. I'll have to thank him for taking such good care of you."

I pull a stool over from the counter and sit. "I can't wait to see you," I tell him.

"I wanted to see you tonight too, but I have to work. I tried, but I couldn't get out it."

"Oh, no. That's too bad."

"I'm sorry, Angel."

"It's okay." I try not to sound as disappointed as I feel. "I understand."

"I promise to make it up to you tomorrow night, okay?"

"I'll look forward to it."

"I really am sorry."

"I know," I say, infusing some cheerfulness into my voice. "An assistant store manager's work is never done."

"Yep, it's always my duty to save the day," he jokes in his best super hero voice and I laugh.

"I guess I will see you tomorrow, then."

"See you tomorrow, Angel."

I can't help feeling disappointed as I hang up the phone.

* * *

Ian's office door is partially opened when I knock.

"Come on in," he calls.

"I just wanted to say thank you for today. I had a great time."

"I enjoyed your company very much. I'm glad you could go with me."

"It was my pleasure." Smiling, I turn to leave.

"So, what do you and Mitch have planned for this evening?"

"Mitch has to work," I answer, turning back to him. "We'll see each other tomorrow."

"He's probably pretty disappointed," Ian says sympathetically.

"He is." I walk over to the window and stand for a moment, taking in the scenic wooded surroundings. "I really love it here."

"I'm glad." He comes over and joins me. "Well, Miss Hughes, since your plans have changed, would you do me the honor of spending the rest of your day with me?"

I grin. "I would be happy to." He smiles back and my heart warms. How I love to see him smile!

* * *

I squeal with both terror and excitement as we hit the giant loop. Ian put his arm around me and I hold the bar tightly as the track goes into a big drop. Ian had wanted to take me someplace to cheer me up and had decided *Ghost Town* in Maggie Valley was the best place to do that. On the way here, I told him I had never been to an amusement park before and he said he loves being able to treat me to something I have always wanted to do.

"How was that?" he asks me as we exit the *Red Devil* roller coaster.

"That was intense!" I tell him as we walk down the ramp.

I have loved every ride and I can tell Ian is having fun just watching me. After sitting for a few minutes to let our stomach settle, we decide to grab something to eat. Perusing the menu board, I tell Ian what I would like, and then I sit at a table and wait for him. He soon brings our food.

A slight frown creases my brow as I glance around. There are numerous stares from people at other tables. I know Ian is used to it, but it really unnerves me.

"Would you like to leave?" he asks me.

"No," I quickly answer, purposely meeting some of the bold stares. "Why?"

"Because you look a little uncomfortable."

"Oh, Ian, I'm sorry. I'm not uncomfortable. I just can't understand why people don't show a little more tact."

"Don't worry about me, Angel. It's been this way for me for a very long time now. It doesn't bother me as much anymore." I watch him looking down at his food, and I sense it really does still bother him a little. "Now you know why I will probably always be alone. People just can't handle this," he says, pointing to his face.

Reaching across the table, I take his hand. "Ian."

He raises his eyes to mine, and for a moment I just look at him. His eyes are beautiful. Everything about him is beautiful to me. "It doesn't matter. It is what's inside that counts." I squeeze his fingers. "And don't ever worry about me being embarrassed to be with you. That will never happen."

I watch his eyes fill and he wipes a finger across them before the tears could fall. "Thank you," he says softly.

"No, thank you," I say, swallowing hard against my own rising emotion. "Thank you for being my friend."

He touches my cheek. "And you for being mine."

* * *

By the time we arrive home, I am exhausted. But before going to bed, I take a minute to write in my journal.

Ian took me for a drive up the Blue Ridge parkway today. It was beautiful and very peaceful. We had a picnic lunch. Then we went for a walk along the stream. When we got back, Mitch called to tell me he had to work late. I wanted so badly to see him. I miss him when we are apart. We plan to go out tomorrow evening.

Ian wanted to cheer me up, so he took me to an amusement park called Ghost Town. I've never had so much fun. We rode ride after ride. Then he treated me to dinner.

I don't know what it is or how to describe it, but it feels so natural to be with him. I feel safe somehow. I am completely drawn to him and I don't know why. And it's not romantic or anything. It's just something I can't describe. I have only known him for two days, yet I feel so close to him.

It's a good feeling.

J. Adams

CHAPTER 6

SCHOOL

*T*he first day of school is a bit overwhelming, but I have no problem finding my classes. I'm pretty excited to have Ian as one of my teachers. Walking into his classroom, I smile and his face lights up. He stands as I approach his desk.

"How are you?" I ask, feeling an unexplainable giddiness.

"I'm great. How has your morning been?"

"Pretty good actually. Although I can't remember ever being this excited about literature. I think it must be the teacher."

Ian laughs. "Well, I'm glad I can make coming to class so exciting for you."

"Me, too."

* * *

Angel grabs a seat up front and Ian gives her a quick wink before opening his roll book. He has never been so excited about starting a new school year, and to say he is glad Angel chose his class is an understatement. When he finally looks up from his book, he almost laughs aloud as over half the guys in the room stretch their necks for a better view of Angel.

My beautiful daughter is going to be the cause of a lot of hernias and pulled muscles this year. He grins as her eyes meet his. *And she's totally oblivious to them all.*

* * *

A girl sitting next to me leans over and whispers, "I think you have a fan club." I casually turn and find all of the guys staring at me. I quickly turn back, a blush burning my cheeks. I glance at Ian and his grin is even wider. "Thanks a lot," I mouth. He makes a face and I release an unladylike snort. Payback is going to be good.

"Do you know Professor Crawford?" the girl asks. "I saw the two of you talking when you came in."

"Yes, I'm renting a room at his home. He is a good friend."

"I think he's a very nice man. I'm Amy," she says, extending her hand to me.

"I'm Angel." I shake her hand and we chat for a few moments until Ian gets class underway.

When class was over, Ian and I have lunch together, and we continue to do so each day. It's something we both look forward to because it is the only time of the day we can always count on to be ours. We talk about everything from school to books, to movies and music, and everything else we can think of.

* * *

My evenings are spent with Mitch. With each day that passes, my love for him grows. Some nights we sit on Ian's porch swing and talk of our dreams for the future. Of course, our plans always include each other. I can't imagine not having Mitch in my life.

I haven't dated many guys, and the few I have gone out with were either too shallow or so into themselves, I couldn't even force myself to enjoy being with them. Before Mitch, I never dreamed I could be so in love with someone, and I look forward to every minute I am able to spend with him.

CHAPTER 7

THE PROPOSAL

Sitting on the front porch steps, I release a contented sigh, securely wrapped in Mitch's arms.

"I'm looking forward to being with you for your first Thanksgiving," he tells me, kissing my brow.

"I am, too."

He smiles, gently stroking my hair. "I love you, Angel."

"And I love you."

Drawing back a little, Mitch reaches into his pocket and pulls out a small box. "Will you marry me?"

I smile tearfully, not even looking at the ring. Pressing a hand to his face, I caress his stubbly jaw. "Yes," I answer breathlessly.

Mitch draws my face closer and presses his lips to mine, favoring me with a warm kiss. "I love you," he whispers again before taking the ring from the box and slipping it on my finger.

"It's beautiful," I say, looking at the heart-shaped solitaire.

"I told my parents I was going to ask you tonight and they were thrilled. They can't wait to have you in our family."

"I feel the same." I have grown to love Mitch's family, and his mother and I have music in common. We both love it and Mitch's sister Lynn never misses an opportunity to ask me to perform some of my songs, which is usually every time they have me over. Sometimes his sisters and their families come to visit when they know I am coming, and after a while, Mitch usually has to pry me away. I adore them all.

"Shall we go and tell them?" I ask, excited to share our news.

Mitch nods. "Let's go. But be prepared to be hugged to death."

I laugh and kiss him. "I'm always prepared for hugs."

* * *

"We're so happy for you guys!" Lynn tells us, hugging me. Mitch's father gives him a bear hug and quickly kisses my cheek. "You couldn't have made a better choice, son." Mitch nods in agreement.

The doorbell rings and Lynn grins widely. "That will be your sisters. I told them you were going to propose to Angel and they were all so excited, they said they were coming over."

Mitch opens the door and we are quickly bombarded with more hugs and kisses.

"I'm so happy for you guys," Heather says excitedly. Of all his sisters, Mitch is closest to her. They are very alike, in both looks and personality. They inherited their mother's light olive complexion and her dark hair. Cindy and Brittany share their father's looks with their auburn hair and fair complexion, as do Mitch's two oldest sisters who live in California. I am looking forward to meeting them as well.

As I relish the love and acceptance of Mitch's family, I think of how welcome I felt when I first met them. They had immediately accepted me as a part of their family, and since I've never had any brothers and sisters, it had been both overwhelming and wonderful.

"Can I see your ring?" Cindy asks and I hold out my hand.

"Oh, it's beautiful!" Brittany gushes.

Sitting with Mitch's family and talking of our plans, my mind drifts to Ian. I can't wait to tell him the news, but at the same time, I am a little sad. Ian seems so alone in the world and I wish he could find happiness with someone. Someone who would see past his outward appearance and look inside his heart. To me, he is beautiful inside and out. He truly deserves to be happy.

* * *

Ian enters Angel's room and places a vase of fresh roses on the dresser. He had planned to just put it there and leave, but instead, he finds himself standing for a moment, taking in all of the personal things Angel brought from England. The room has so much of her in it, it's as if she has lived here forever. He walks over to the chair in the corner where the Raggedy Ann doll he had given her for her first birthday sits. Smiling, he picks up the doll, and then closes his eyes and holds it to his chest, wishing he could get back all the years he missed with his little girl.

Placing the doll back in the chair, he stands to leave when the photo album catches his eye. He's seen it there many times before, but he never dared to open it for fear of the painful memories it is sure to bring.

Angel treasures the pictures of her parents, and each time she leaves the house, Ian is presented with the opportunity to look through the album, but he has fought the urge, having long since forgotten the way he once looked. More than just being afraid of seeing his past self, he isn't sure if he can handle seeing the pictures of his wife.

He again glances at the album on the stand and starts backing towards the door, but when his hand touches the knob, he stops, unable to fight the pull. Giving in, he makes his way back to the nightstand and sits on the edge of the bed with the book.

Taking a deep breath, he opens it. On the first page is a picture of Angel on her first birthday. Ian swallows hard at the lump in his throat. The picture brings back so clearly the day he and Emma said goodbye to their little girl.

He closed his eyes, holding his breath as he turns the page. Opening them, his gaze drops and tears quickly streaked his face. A sob tears from his throat as he gazes at his beloved Emma's face. His heart aches as the memories of their life together come flooding back. He misses her so much more than he thought. Looking at the photo a moment longer, he forces himself to turn to the next page.

Holding the back of his hand to his mouth, he bites down as he takes in the vision of the man he once was. His blond hair was a little longer then, and the dimples he can no longer see were very prominent.

Unable to look any longer, he quickly closes the book, placing it back on the nightstand and sits with his head in his hands. "God," he cries, "please help me! This hurts so much. Please help me!"

* * *

Mitch drops me off at 10:45. When I enter the house, Ian is sitting in the living room, seemingly lost in his thoughts. He looks up as I approach.

"I didn't even hear you come in."

"I know. You look so far away." I sit next to him and squeeze his hand gently. "What is it?"

"Nothing really," he says, closing his hand over mine. "I just have a lot on my mind."

"Is there anything I can do?"

"No, I'm fine." He smiles, but I know it's only to keep me from worrying. "So, how was your night with Mitch?"

"It was wonderful!" I answer, positively giddy.

"Well, you look pretty excited. What did you two do?" When my grin widens, he laughs. "Okay, now you've really got me curious."

I'm dying to tell him and I hope he will be as excited for me as I am. "Well, we talked about things and . . . he asked me to marry him."

Ian smiles, his eyes shining. "Oh, Angel, that's so wonderful!"he says, hugging me. "I'm so happy for you two. You were made for each other."

"Thanks. I think so, too."

"You know, I knew he was going to ask you soon."

"Oh, you did?"

"Definitely."

"How did you know," I ask, laughing.

"Well, a young man gets a certain look in his eyes when he is about to propose. It's that 'I-love-her-so-much, I can't-live-without-her-so-I-had-better-ask-her-to-marry-me, but-I-am-scared-to-death' kind of look."

We both start laughing so hard, we can't stop. By the time we manage to, my side hurts. How I love hearing him laugh! Sometimes he seems so sad and I love doing or saying something to make him smile. Sobering, I look into his eyes and all at once, emotion wells up inside me and I have no idea why. I wrap my arms around his neck, hugging him tightly. "I love you, Ian."

* * *

Angel's display of emotion leaves Ian speechless. He doesn't know what is happening. He only knows he doesn't ever want it to end. Holding her close, he softly strokes her hair, which is now moist from his tears. "I love you, too, my Angel. I love you too."

J. Adams

CHAPTER 8

A SURPRISE AND DISCOVERY

*M*itch and I plan our wedding for February and I call my aunt to tell her the news, as well as inform her I will be coming home for Christmas. Aunt Elaine is ecstatic about the wedding and thrilled I will be in England for Christmas.

Wanting to get everything done as soon as we can, we pick out invitations, made up our guest list and start planning the reception.

One morning after Ian and I finish breakfast, he tells me he has a surprise for me. He puts on his coat and helps me into mine. "Where are we going?" I ask as he opens the car door.

"It's a surprise, remember?" He grins, pulling out of the driveway.

"Oh, come on, Ian, tell me. Please?"

"Nope. You'll just have to wait." My lips form a pout and he laughs. "Sorry, but that's not going to work because I have a will of iron." When I give him my puppy dog eyes, he holds up a hand. "No fair, Angel."

"I know," I say, "but I will wait."

After a twenty minute drive, Ian heaves a sigh of relief as we reach our destination. "We made it and I didn't break."

"It's a bridal shop," I say, surprised.

"Yes, it is."

"But . . . why are we here?"

Ian jumps out of the car and quickly opens my door. "We are here, my dear, to buy you a wedding dress."

"I can't let you do that."

"Yes, you can."

"No, I can't," I argue.

* * *

Ian gently places his hands on her shoulders. "Angel, you have no idea how much happiness you have brought into my life. I really want to do this for you. Please let me." *Let me be your father and do what fathers do for their daughters.*

"But it's so much."

"Don't you worry about that."

"But . . ."

"No buts," he interrupts before she can say another word. He takes her hand, pulling her into the store.

* * *

"Wow! They are all so beautiful!" I say, looking at some of the more modest dresses.

"May I help you?" the sales woman asks, emerging from the back room.

"Yes," Ian answers, turning to her. "This young lady would like to buy a wedding dress."

I watch the woman quickly mask her shock upon seeing Ian. I can tell he notices but pretends not to.

"Would you like to try a few on?" she asks me, nervously glancing at Ian, then away again.

"Yes, I would," I answer, annoyed by her obvious discomfort. I give Ian's hand a squeeze and he forces a smile.

I show the woman the dresses I want to try on and she quickly takes them into one of the large dressing rooms. Ian sits in one of the nearby chairs and flips through a bridal magazine while I change.

I try on a princess gown. It had caught my eye before the others. The silky material feels elegant and luxurious against my skin.

"Well, what do you think?" I ask, exiting the dressing room and walking over to the full length mirror by Ian.

Ian looked up from the magazine, saying nothing for a moment, but his expression speaks volumes. "Mitch will not be able to take his eyes off you. Neither will anyone else. You look beautiful."

"Thank you," I tell him, a blush heating my cheeks. I turn around in front of the large mirror, admiring the dress, feeling like Cinderella. "I really love this one. I think Mitch will too."

"I know he will," Ian says, still gazing at me. I smile at the sales woman as she approaches.

"You know, I don't think I need to try on the other dresses. I would like this one."

"You do look very pretty in it," the woman tells me. "It is such a perfect fit, I don't think it will require alterations."

* * *

While Angel heads back to the dressing room to change, Ian follows the woman to the counter to pay for the dress.

"Are there going to be bridesmaids," she asks, printing up the receipt. She averts her eyes and it is obvious to Ian she is doing her best to avoid looking at him.

"I don't know. I will have to ask her."

"Well, if she does need dresses for bridesmaids, we have some very pretty ones that would coordinate well with the gown she has chosen." The woman looks at him briefly as she tells him the total. Ian pays her and she gives him the receipt.

* * *

Standing at the counter, the woman asks me to wait while she puts the dress in a box.

"I'll wait for you in the car," Ian whispers, leaving before I can protest.

The sales woman returns and hands the box to me. "As I mentioned to the gentleman, if you need bridesmaids dresses, we have a great selection."

"Thank you," I say as cordially as I can. I know Ian is upset and I know it is because of this woman. I have grown very defensive and protective of him and it irritates me when people look at him and treat him like he has the plague. Swallowing my anger, I thank the woman for her help and leave.

I get in the car and place my dress in the back seat. Then I wrap my arms around Ian's neck and kiss his cheek. "Thank you so much."

"You're welcome," he says with a smile that doesn't seem to reach his eyes.

"Are you okay?"

"Yes, I'm fine." He starts the car and pulls out of the parking lot.

"So, what are your plans for today?" he asks me.

"Well, later this afternoon I am going to see Mitch's sister, Cindy. Her little boy has been sick."

"I hope it's nothing serious," Ian says, concerned.

"Actually, he's had pneumonia, but he's doing a lot better."

"That's good. I know how hard that can be on little kids. I had it when I was young and it was no fun."

"Really? So did I."

Ian's eyes widen, surprising me. "You had pneumonia?"

"Yes, when I was five."

"Your aunt must have been pretty worried."

"She was. I was in the hospital for over a week. It was also during that time that I lost part of my hearing."

"What?"

I am startled by the shocked look on his face. "I'm sorry, I thought I mentioned it to you. I lost about thirty-five percent of my hearing in my right ear. I hear okay, but I always try to look directly at people when I talk to them."

"You're partially deaf, yet you sing and play beautifully. You have been very blessed."

"Thank you."

"Did you feel afraid, or alone," he asks and I can hear the emotion in his voice.

"A little. But my aunt stayed with me a lot, and there were always nurses checking in on me."

Ian nodded, saying nothing more.

Before we know it, we are pulling into the driveway. Ian carries my dress up and places it on my bed.

"Thank you again," I say, hugging him before he turns to leave.

He returns my embrace and rests his chin on top of my head. "You're very welcome."

Detecting sudden note of sadness in his voice, I tighten my embrace.

"I have some phone calls to make." He presses a kiss to my brow and pulls away. "I'll see you in a little while."

I watch him leave the room, closing the door behind him, and I can't help wondering what happened to bring about such sadness.

Oh, how I wish I could read your mind, Ian Crawford!

* * *

Louise takes me Christmas shopping. I've already shopped for Mitch, his family, and my aunt, and I've finished a special present for Ian. It is something I have been working on for a while. But I need Louise to give me some ideas of other things I can give him as well.

I decide on a tie and a dress shirt for work and a couple of beautiful, framed paintings of picturesque landscapes. I know Ian will love them and I plan to give them to him a few days before I leave for England. This is the first time I've had this much fun Christmas shopping.

After we're done, we have lunch and talk more about Ian. I'm excited to go home, but leaving Ian is harder than I thought it would be. We've become so close over the months my heart swells to think about how happy I feel just being around him. I hate the thought of him being alone.

My thoughts must be written in my expression because Louise places her hand over mine and says, "Ian is going to miss you a lot."

I sigh. "I'm going to miss him, too. More than I ever imagined. He's been like a father to me. I can't tell you how good that feels, how happy I've been. I mean, my childhood was a good one and I have been blessed with a good life, but a part of me has always felt a little empty. Ian fills that part."

Louise smiles and I have to wonder about the emotion I see in her eyes. "Ian loves you very much, and I'm so glad you came to stay."

"I am as well." I squeeze her hand back. "I count myself blessed to be a part of your son's life."

* * *

Sitting on the porch swing, I rock back and forth, watching the puffs of my breath escape into the cold air. I hug myself tightly to relieve some of the cold as thoughts about my upcoming trip consume my mind. I am excited to see Aunt Elaine again, but it hurts to think of being away from Mitch, even more so than Ian. They are the two men I love most in the world and I won't be spending Christmas with either.

"There you are," Ian says coming out on the porch.

"Hi."

"What are you doing out here?" he asks, sitting next to me on the swing.

"Oh, just thinking."

"About?"

"You."

"Me?" he asks, surprised. "What about me?" He put his arm around me and I nuzzled close, resting my head against his shoulder.

"I was just thinking about how much I am going to miss you when I leave."

* * *

Ian feels emotion welling up in him again. He can't believe how close they have become and the thought of being away from her is tearing him apart. He tightens his arm around her, kissing her forehead. "I'm going to miss you too, but two weeks isn't long," he says, even though it will feel like an eternity to him. It seems like it was just yesterday that she came into his life, and the thought of spending Christmas away from her hurts more than words could express. He has already missed too many Christmases in her life. "We still have this week."

She nods, smiling up at him. "I love you."

"And I love you." Rocking the porch swing, he silently relishes the sound of the three words he will never tire of hearing.

CHAPTER 9

THE DREAM

*W*hen Ian awakens the next morning, his thoughts are of Angel and Mitch. His night had been consumed with dreaming the same dream over and over again.

In the dream he was sitting on a theater stage, tied to a chair, and the audience was full of laughing people. They were laughing at *him*. They started throwing things at him. He couldn't tell exactly what they were throwing, but the objects were hard.

Just as he'd starting to lose consciousness from being hit repeatedly, he saw two people emerge from the crowd. As they came closer to the stage he recognized them. It was Angel and Mitch. They walked up onto the stage and proceeded to untie him. Frightened, he looked into Angel's eyes and the love he saw in them warmed his whole being. He turned to look at Mitch and saw the same love. And even though they were also being hit by the objects, the look of love and peace never left their faces.

Ian lays back on the pillows and raises his eyes heavenward, knowing all too well what the dream meant. And he knows what he needs to do. With shaking hands he reaches for the phone and begins to dial.

"Hi, . . .Mitch, it's Ian. I need to come and see you this morning. There's something I need to talk to you about."

* * *

Ian holds his hands together for a moment and tries to keep them from shaking. He glances at Mitch as he waits patiently. Finally ready to begin, Ian tries to choose his words carefully.

"First, I need to apologize to you."

"Apologize to me? Mitch looks puzzled. "Why?"

"Because I did something very wrong, and once I tell you what it is, I hope you will be able to find it in your heart to forgive me." When Mitch stays silent, Ian continues.

"What I am about to tell you must remain for now, strictly between you and me. You can't tell anyone, especially Angel."

"Okay, now you've really got me curious. I'm listening."

Ian takes a deep breath. "Do you remember how excited I was when you told me you were going to England for that architecture class?"

"Yes. You were even more excited than I was. And when I said it was in London, you were ecstatic."

"I know. There was a reason for that." He pauses for a moment or two. "You see . . . I knew there was a chance you would . . . that you would meet Angel."

Mitch looked confused. "Angel? What do you mean?"

Ian tries to find an easy way to say it, but there isn't an easier way except to just come straight out with it. He sighs deeply. "Angel is my daughter."

Mitch stares at him blankly for a moment. "Did you just say Angel is your daughter?"

Ian looks down and nods.

"But, that's impossible. Her father is . . ."

Ian looks up just as Mitch's gaze takes in his scarred face for the first time in a long time, and saw the reality of his words suddenly hit home.

"The plane crash. That's how you were burned. You . . . you never told me exactly how it happened. Now I know." Mitch is quiet and Ian can see a million thoughts and emotions running through the young man's mind. "Why?" Mitch finally asks sadly.

Ian sits down on the sofa, and with a trembling voice, tells him the whole story. By the time he is finished, the confusion, anger and betrayal he'd seen etched in Mitch's features a moment before, have melted into a look of loving compassion and understanding.

"I'm sorry, Mitch. You have been a good friend to me. I have been completely dishonest with you and I will regret betraying your trust for the rest of my life. Do you think you could ever forgive me?"

Mitch says nothing for a moment. Standing, he pulls Ian up into a tight embrace. After a moment, he releases him and says, "I do forgive you, and I understand."

Ian is relieved beyond words and his heart is full of gratitude. Mitch means the world to him and to lose his friendship would be devastating.

Mitch places a hand on Ian's shoulder. "You have to tell Angel."

This is a truth Ian has always known, no matter how much he has tried to deny it. "It will hurt her," he says, rubbing his eyes before the tears can fall. "I never wanted to hurt her."

"I know you don't, and it *will* hurt, at first. I'm sure she will feel a lot of things. But she loves you. There's no mistaking that. And now that I know the truth, I can understand why you two bonded so quickly and easily."

"I love her so much."

"I know you do. It might be hard, but she will eventually understand, and she will forgive you. It's a chance you are going to have to take."

Ian looks up wearily. "She is everything to me."

"Then you have to tell her."

"She's leaving in less than a week."

"Then that doesn't give you much time."

Ian shakes his head. " I don't know if I can– "

"Hey," Mitch interrupts, "do you have a valid passport?"

"Yes," Ian answers. "Why?"

"Why don't you tag along with her to England?"

Ian's mouth drops open. "No, I couldn't."

"Why not? I bet Angel would love to have you go. You can get to know your wife's aunt again. And I think the country of your birth would be the perfect place to tell your daughter she still has a father."

"Maybe you're right," he says, hope entering his being.

"I can see God's hand in all of this, Ian. I know I'm right."

* * *

Every few minutes I look out the front window. I have been waiting all morning for Ian to get back. I was actually surprised to find him gone this morning when I came down for breakfast and hoped he would be back by now. I need to ask him something I should have asked weeks before, and now I'm so excited about it, I can hardly keep still.

Glancing down at my watch again, I finally decide to go back up to my room when I see him pull into the driveway.

"Hi," I say as he comes through the door.

"Hi."

Taking his hand, I pull him into the living room. "I have something to ask you."

"Okay, but, there's something I need to ask you, too."

We sit down on the sofa. "Okay, you first," I say.

Ian hesitates a moment. "Do you think your Aunt would mind having an unexpected guest?"

I gasp. "Do you mean . . .?"

"Yes. I would like to go with you, if it's okay. I mean I don't . . ."

Before he can even finish, I throw my arms around him, knocking him back on the couch. I am completely ecstatic. "Of course it's okay! I was going to ask you to come. I'm so excited!"

* * *

"I am, too," Ian says holding his daughter close. He truly is excited—excited and scared. He also knows there is no turning back now. Tightening his embrace, he closes his eyes.

What did I just get myself into?

CHAPTER 10

GOING HOME

*W*atching passengers walk through the security gate, Elaine anxiously waits for Angel. She can't wait to see her and is overjoyed to hear she is bringing a friend. Angel told her all about Ian and Elaine is looking forward to getting to know this man her niece is so taken with.

"Auntie!" Angel calls as she comes through the gate and runs into the older woman's embrace.

"Oh, Angel, it's so good to see you!" Elaine says, hugging her tightly. "I have missed you so much."

"I've missed you."

* * *

Ian stands back watching them. He can't get over how young Elaine still looks. Her hair is grayer, but her face hasn't aged at all. He has not seen her in over twenty years, and he still feels more love for her than he imagined. She raised his daughter well and he will never be able to repay her for that.

"This is Ian Crawford," Angel says, taking his hand and pulling him over to them. "Ian, this is my Aunt Elaine."

"It is a pleasure to meet you Mr. Crawford," Elaine says, extending her hand.

"The pleasure is mine and please, call me Ian."

"Is this your first time in England, Ian?"

"Actually, I have been to London, but it was a long time ago." He sees the surprised look on Angel's face and squeezes her hand. "It was a very, very long time ago."

"Well, I hope you will enjoy your time here."

"Oh, I'm going to make sure of it," Angel says, looping her arm through his.

* * *

Sighing, I take in the sights and sounds of the city. I have missed England so much. Glancing at Ian, I am surprised by the emotion I see in his eyes as he takes in the surroundings, and I can't help wondering what kind of memories London holds for him.

I smile as we pull up in front of my family flat, happy to be back. Ian grabs our luggage and we head inside.

* * *

Even though Ian still knows every corner of the house, it isn't hard for him to pretend he hasn't been there before. It's been a long time since he's seen the place and he feels as if he is seeing it for the first time. Angel takes him to the guest room, which was once her room. She tells him that when she turned ten, she and Elaine moved her things into her parent's room. It always helped her to feel closer to them.

"I hope you will be comfortable here," she says.

"I'm sure I will. It's a beautiful room."

"Thanks."

"Well, why don't I unpack and give you and your aunt time to catch up."

"All right. Is there anything you need?"

"No, I'm fine. Thank you."

"You're welcome," she says, smiling. "I'm so glad you are here." She hugs him and kisses his cheek before leaving the room, closing the door behind her.

Finally alone, Ian sits on the bed, sighing as he looks around the room. There are so many memories here. He lays back on the pillows and thinks about all of the hours he'd spent in this room, rocking Angel to sleep and singing to her. He ponders all of the missed time and opportunities he can never get back.

Suddenly, a wave of fear sweeps over him. He knows he will have to tell Angel the truth, but again he can't help wondering if he can really go through with it. Slipping to his knees beside the bed, he begins to pray. When he is done, he remains on his knees a few minutes longer, and for the first time in a long time, he feels peace. He knows everything will work out.

I'll tell her tomorrow.

* * *

My aunt and I talk while I unpack.

"Your friend Ian is very nice. It is easy to see how close you two are."

"We *are* very close," I agree. "It has been wonderful having him in my life."

"I am glad he has been so good for you." Elaine is silent for a moment, then she asks, "Did he ever tell you what happened to him, how he was hurt?"

"He's never really discussed it with me. He just said it happened a long time ago."

"It must have been a pretty bad accident. He has the most beautiful eyes, though. They are just as blue as your father's eyes were, and yours."

"Yes, I noticed his eyes when I first met him, too."

Putting the empty suitcase on the floor, I sit on the bed and Elaine sits beside me.

"You know, from the moment I met Ian, I felt drawn to him and I can't explain why. After a while I stopped trying to analyze it." I turn to Elaine and take her hand. "You raised me and were there for me. I will always love you and be grateful to you for everything.

But there was always an empty space in my heart. Mitch filled a big part of it and I can't imagine not having him in my life, but I needed more. Ian has made everything complete. I know my parents would love him as much as I do."

Elaine touches my cheek. "You were pretty happy growing up, but I knew there were times when you needed more. You always tried to keep those sad times hidden, but I knew. I am glad you have found so much happiness."

"So am I," I say, hugging her. "So am I."

CHAPTER 11

A FAMILIAR FACE

Dinner is ready, you two." Elaine calls from the kitchen. Angel and Ian head to the dining room and seat themselves.

"Everything looks wonderful," Ian tells Elaine.

"Thank you."

Elaine asks Angel to say the blessing on the food, and as she does, Elaine opens her eyes a little and looks at Ian. She normally would never do such a thing, but she is starting to sense something familiar about him.

She hadn't thought about it when she first met him, but after talking with him and getting to know him a little more, there is definitely something about him she recognizes. When Angel closes the blessing, Elaine quickly lowers her head and says amen.

"Ian, is your mother going to be spending Christmas alone?" Elaine asks.

Ian takes a piece of chicken from the tray. "No, she will be spending the holidays with a good friend and her family."

"From what you have told me about her, she sounds like a wonderful person. I hope I'll have the opportunity to meet her one day."

"I hope you will, too," he says with a smile. "She is a very special woman. She has been the best mother I could ever ask for."

* * *

"Are you okay, Ian?" I ask, noticing the far away look in his eyes.

"Oh, I'm fine," he answers. "I just hope she's doing okay."

"I'm sure she is," I assure him.

Elaine cooked so much food that by the time we are all done, I am so stuffed I can't move.

"Wow, I sure could use a wheel barrel about now," I say to Ian and he laughs. We begin clearing the table and helping to put things away. Ian and I volunteer to do the dishes since Aunt Elaine had done all of the cooking.

Later in the evening, we pop popcorn and make hot chocolate for our tree trimming party. Aunt Elaine had waited to decorate the tree until I came because it's has always been one of the most exciting parts of Christmas for me.

Aunt Elaine puts on a Christmas CD while Ian and I hang the lights on the tree. It takes us a while, but we finally get them arranged to our satisfaction. My aunt helps us hang the ornaments.

"It is so beautiful," I say, gazing at the finished tree. Ian put his arm around me. "I don't think I have ever enjoyed decorating a tree more," I tell him, returning his embrace and he kisses my brow.

"I love you, my Angel."

"I love you too."

* * *

As Elaine silently watches this exchange, she looks at Ian, then at Angel, and back at Ian again. She takes in his scarred face, and then his eyes. Those eyes! Those beautiful eyes are becoming shockingly familiar. Elaine presses a hand to her chest, momentarily feeling like she can't breathe.

"Are you okay, Auntie?" Angel asks.

"Oh, I'm fine," Elaine answers, her voice calm. "I just remembered I need to make a phone call. I will be right back." She quickly heads to the kitchen. Grabbing the edge of the counter, she holds on and tries to get her thoughts together.

No! It couldn't be! He died!

Elaine shakes her head, trying to straighten her thoughts. She keeps telling herself, *It couldn't possibly be!* Then she stops. Her eyes grow large as another realization dawns on her. *They never recovered his body. They found Emma, but, they never found . . .* "Shane," she whispers.

Taking a deep breath, she stands at the counter another moment to compose herself before rejoining Angel and Ian.

"Is everything okay?" Angel asks as Elaine enters the living room.

"Yes, everything is fine. It was a very important phone call and I should have made it earlier. I've . . . I've been so excited to have you home, I guess it just slipped my mind."

"It's good you remembered," Ian says, smiling at her. She smiles back and sits in the large recliner across from them.

"So, tell me, Ian, how long ago were you in England?" Elaine asks casually.

He raises the cup of hot chocolate to his lips, hesitating to answer. "It was too long ago to remember," he says lightly. As he places his cup on the table, he looks up to find her staring at him intently, which makes him a little nervous.

"Well, we will make sure you see all of the sights and make this a memorable visit for you."

"I'm sure it will be," he says, looking at Angel. She smiles, squeezing his hand.

"I am grateful to you for all you have done for Angel," Elaine continues. Then she adds, "You have been like a father to her. The father she has always wanted."

Ian tries to mask the momentary pain he is sure flashes in his eyes. "And she has been like a daughter to me."

After a while, Ian can't help noticing the strange looks Elaine is giving him, and the uneasy feeling he has fought for the most part returns, only now it is even stronger.

Why does she keep looking at me like that? he wonders. *I'm used to people staring, used to the odd looks. But, she didn't look at me like that in the beginning. So, why would she . . .* He looks over at her. Their eyes meet and in an instant, he knows the answer. She knows who he is. Even after all this time, she recognizes him.

Angel yawns. "I think I'm going to head up to bed."

Ian pulls his eyes from Elaine. "I'm sure you must be tired after our long flight, and we have been going non stop since we arrived. Why don't you go on up and I will help your aunt put everything away."

"Are you sure?"

"Yes, you go on ahead."

Ian takes in Elaine's look of surprise. There is no running away from this and he is determined to face it head on. Angel kisses them both good night and leaves them standing in silence.

Ian immediately takes two of the cups to the kitchen. Elaine picks up the remaining cup and the half empty bowl of popcorn and follows him, neither of them uttering a word. When Ian places the cups in the sink, Elaine approaches him. Keeping his head down, he silently prays. When he finally meets her eyes, his own are moist and he finally breaks the silence.

"I need to explain." His words are almost a whisper.

Elaine looks at his face. "You are Shane, aren't you?"

"Yes," he answers, sorrow filling his pleading eyes.

She pulled a chair from the table and sits. Ian also grabs a chair, turning to face her and places his hand on hers, his heart aching when she begins to cry. After a moment, she wipes her eyes.

"Why?" is all she asks. "Why did you stay away? Angel is your only child. Why didn't you come back?"

"Because of this," he says, pointing to his tear-streaked face. "She deserved a normal father."

"Oh, Shane!" she cries softly, squeezing his hand.

"I'm sorry, Elaine. I'm so sorry. I know now that it was wrong and I can't change the past. But I will do everything in my power to make things right. Please forgive me."

"Oh, Shane," she cries once more and embraces him. "I can't believe you are really here! I can't believe you are alive!" She drew back to look at him. "You have to tell Angel. She loves you so much and she deserves to know you are really her father."

"I know. That's why I came with her. I know it's time. I plan to tell her tomorrow. I only hope she will be able to forgive me."

"I know Angel, and I know she will come to understand. But, you need to understand, too. Your outward appearance means nothing. It is what's in your heart that means everything, especially to her."

Ian smiles, his heart bursting with love for this woman who had meant the world to he and Emma.

Elaine stood, her teary smile wide. "How about I make us some more hot chocolate? This is going to be a long night, because I want to know everything."

J. Adams

CHAPTER 12

DAY OF TRUTH

Wake up, sleepy head," Ian says as he set the tray down beside Angel's bed. He had gotten up early and prepared breakfast for her, determined to make this Christmas Eve day as special as he possibly can, because he knows what he will tell her sometime today day will definitely make it a day she will never forget. He just hopes it will be in a good way.

"This is a surprise," she says sleepily.

He kisses her cheek. "Happy Christmas Eve."

"Thank you," she says, rubbing her eyes. "Happy Christmas Eve to you, too." She sits up and pushes the hair away from her face. Ian places the tray over her lap.

"Wow, this looks great! Thank you."

"You're welcome."

"I hope Auntie doesn't yell at you too much for raiding her kitchen," she says, teasing.

Ian chuckles. "Actually, she didn't mind at all. In fact, she helped me."

"I'm glad you two are getting along well. I told her before we came that she would love you as much as I do."

His expression is somber. "I don't know if anyone will ever love me as much as you do, and it really doesn't matter." He presses a hand to her cheek. "You mean more to me than anything else in this world. I wanted you to know that, Angel, and believe it. Nothing else matters." He smiles. "I just needed to tell you that."

* * *

"Thank you. I'm glad you did." Ian's sudden display of emotion touches my heart. I press a hand against his wet cheek. "And I can't imagine not having you in my life."

"Okay," he said, wiping his face. "Eat up now. We have a big day ahead of us. We are going to see all of London today so, we had better get a move on."

I laugh at his enthusiasm. "Whatever you say."

I finish my breakfast, then quickly shower and dress, all the while worrying about Ian. I have seen sadness in his eyes many times, but this time his eyes seemed to hold an emotion I have never seen in them—fear. But what could he possibly be afraid of?

By the time I am done, Ian has already packed a picnic lunch and is pacing while waiting for me.

Elaine gives me her car keys and quickly kisses my cheek before rushing us out the door.

* * *

Ian and Angel spend the entire morning visiting the historical sites of Westminster Abbey and Buckingham Palace. He truly has missed England. Later in the afternoon they stop at a park and eat their picnic lunch. The park is right across the street from the cemetery where Emma is buried. Tears fill his eyes as his gaze lingers in that direction.

"Are you okay?" Angel asks.

He knows it is time to tell her the truth. He has prayed throughout the day that when the time came, he would be able to go through with it.

"Angel, would you show me your mother's grave? I know your father was never found, but, I would like to see where your mother is buried."

"I would be happy to," she answers, looking at him curiously. They finish eating and pack everything into the basket, and head to the car.

"Ian, is there is something wrong? Please tell me. You know you can tell me anything."

He lovingly places a hand on her cheek, smiling sadly. "Let's go, my Angel. I will tell you everything."

* * *

The solemn sound of Ian's words lingers in the air as I pull into the cemetery. As we walk, I glance at him, anxious to know what he could be holding inside that would cause him so much pain. Taking his hand, I lead him to my mother's grave.

* * *

Ian's heart pounds harder with each step. By the time they reach Emma's grave, he finds it hard to breathe. Gazing down at the grave of his beloved wife, each and every memory he shared with her floods his mind. He looks at Angel standing next to him with concern written across her face, and he pulls her into his embrace, desperation filling him. He holds her in silence, trying to think of how to begin. After a few moments he draws back and takes her hands in his.

"Angel, I need to tell you something."

* * *

"Okay," I say, hoping he is finally going to open up to me. I have never been as concerned for someone as I am for him and it is killing me to see him so distraught. I watch him swallow hard.

"Angel . . . sometimes when you love someone, you make decisions you feel are in that person's best interest, and sometimes it's very painful. Then after a while you start to question whether the decision was the right one, and by the time you realize it wasn't, you are convinced it's too late to do anything about it."

I squeeze his hand "It's never too late," I said softly.

"Oh, Angel," he say with a small sob, "I pray it's not too late."

I glimpse the fear returning to his face, as well as pain. "Please tell me, Ian."

"Angel, I need to tell you a story. It's a story of a man who had a wife and a little girl he loved more than anything.

"One day this man and his wife kissed their little girl goodbye and boarded a plane. She never saw them again. The plane went down and there was an explosion before it crashed. Everyone on the plane was killed except for the man, and no one knew he was alive."

A sudden queasiness enters me and I know he senses it because his voice is shaky as he quickly continues. "This man was found miles away and was taken to the hospital. He was taken care of by a kind nurse and her husband who was a doctor. For weeks, the man lay in the hospital, his hands . . . and face covered in bandages, with no memory of who he was or what had happened."

Ian holds my shaking hands tighter, his eyes never leaving mine.

"When the man finally regained his memory, it was as if all of it had been a bad dream, until he looked in the mirror and saw his face."

My heart is threatening to pound through my chest as fragments of understanding start to fall into place. "Ian," I say, my voice quivering, "what are you telling me?"

He continues. "Once the man saw his face, he thought of his daughter and knew he couldn't go back. He knew he would forever be thought of as a freak and he couldn't do that to his little girl. She deserved a normal parent. Someone who could take her places, someone she would not be ashamed to be seen with. So, with the help of the couple that took care of him, he made a new life for himself, never telling them about his daughter. He tried to be happy, but each day he was away from her brought more pain than he ever thought possible. There wasn't a day he didn't think about his little girl or a night he didn't ache to hold her in his arms and rock her to sleep."

Lowering my head, I silently cry. The pain inside me is so intense, I can barely think. I pull my hands from his and move away from him.

He quickly continues. "One day the man's friend enrolled in an architecture class in the city where his daughter lived, and he was overjoyed. He knew there was a chance his friend would meet his daughter. Each day the man prayed for that, and one day it happened. Not only did he meet her, he fell in love with her. Before coming home, the man convinced him to talk her into coming to the states to go to school." Ian pauses, a soft sob escaping him. "His friend was totally unaware that he was being used. The man felt guilty for that, but he was desperate to see his daughter, to be near her. He didn't want her to know he was her father because of the way he looked, so he became her friend. And with each passing day, the love he felt for her grew."

My feelings are a mass of confusion, and as hard as I try to straighten them out in my head, I don't know how to feel. Here is a man I have considered my dearest friend, someone I can talk to about anything. From the moment I met him, I felt a closeness to him I couldn't explain and I had no idea why. Now I do.

He is my father.

When Ian says nothing more, I break the silence. "I can't tell you how many times I have daydreamed about you being my father. You were everything I could ever want in a father, and I grew to love you so much. And now to find out after all this time . . ."

I abruptly turn and walked back to the car.

* * *

Ian stands at Emma's grave a moment longer, weeping silently. He dries his eyes and whispers, "God, please help me. Please don't let me lose her."

He walks back to the car and gets in. Angel immediately starts the engine and pulls away from the curb. Ian tries to read her face, but he can't.

"Please talk to me," he pleads.

Angel wipes away a stray tear. "I can't." Her voice is toneless.

"I know you need time to absorb everything." When she doesn't acknowledge him, he says nothing more. They ride home in silence.

As they get out of the car to go inside, Angel turns to him. "Does Auntie know?"

Ian nods. "I told her last night, but she had already figured it out."

He follows Angel into the house and Elaine is waiting for them. Angel rushes to her room.

Elaine puts her hand on Ian's shoulder. "Give her time. Everything will work out."

Ian wearily hangs his head. "I hurt her so much. How could I hurt her like that?" He rubs his eyes. "If I lose her now after all this time, I don't know what I'll do. I love her so much."

"And she loves you. Just have faith. Everything will be okay.

CHAPTER 13

THE LOVE I SEE

I sit in a corner of my room, trying understand. I know why Ian made the choice he did, but I am still angry with him.

I was his daughter, his only child, and he never came back for me! How could he say he loved me and do that? I mentally ask this over and over again. Taking a deep breath, I close my eyes as memories of the time we've spent together flood my mind.

I think back to the first day we met and how there was an instant connection between us. It had been so wonderful to have someone I could turn to like a father. Then I think about all the times I saw pain in Ian's eyes.

It is because of that pain I know he loves me, and now that I know the truth, so many things begin to fall into place.

Now everything makes sense.

* * *

Later in the evening, Ian opens the bedroom door to find Angel standing there with swollen red eyes that match his own. Saying nothing, he moves aside for her to enter, then quickly closes the door and goes to her. When she looks at him, her bottom lip begins to tremble.

"You should have come back. It wouldn't have mattered to me. I was young, but I needed you and you let me think . . . you let me think you were dead."

"I'm sorry," he whispers, tears streaming down his face. "I'm so sorry. Please forgive me. I made a mistake and I will regret it for the rest of my life, but you have always been my Angel, and you always will be. I love you so much, baby." He didn't know what else to say.

"I love you, too," she sobs. "And I always will." Closing the space between them, she steps into his arms.

A dam breaks inside Ian and all the years of pain and hurt come pouring out. His body wracking with sobs, he slowly sinks to his knees and Angel drops to the floor with him, holding and rocking him.

"It's okay," she whispers. "I forgive you, Dad. It's okay."

Her words are the sweetest he has ever heard.

* * *

Ian seats himself next to me on the piano bench. I glance over at Elaine sitting in a chair across from us and smile.

"I finished this song last week and a few minutes ago I changed some of the lyrics. I wanted to give you something special for Christmas. I hope you like it.

With a heart full of love for my father, I begin, hoping he will feel that love.

As I repeat the chorus a final time, I send a prayer of thanks to the heavens, for I have truly been blessed.

*In your eyes I see all the wonders
of the world,
all the lifelong love a fathers' sown
for his not so little girl.
For the Father of us all has granted
a special gift to me,
He has blessed with the knowledge
of forever. Your daughter I will always
be. It's the love that's in your eyes
I see.*

About the Author

J. Adams has written books in different genres, but her main focus is inspirational interracial romance. She is a motivational speaker to both youth and adult audiences. In her spare time (when she has any) you can find her curled up with a good book and a healthy stash of orange Tic Tacs.

She and her family reside in Utah.

Email: jewela40@gmail.com

Websites:

gisellesrain.weebly.com

JewelAdams.com

J. Adams